PAPER AIRPLANES OF LOVE

A Simple Form of Love

Written by: **C.M. Rossi**

Illustrated by: **Abby Musial**

I'll never forget the day
I looked to the sky, when a simply
folded paper airplane flew by.

I jumped from my swing to follow
it down, but instead it kept sailing
and led me through town.

Past buildings and churches, shops and my school.
The plane wasn't stopping, it almost seemed cruel!

A barrier finally was in its way.
A tree in the park was where it would lay.

I started to climb,
needing to see it at last ...

... and reached with every finger, took hold and fell fast!
The airplane looked tired, all crumpled and dirty.
It had lost its straight lines and didn't seem very sturdy.

I unfolded it carefully, anxious to see, a little red peeked out,
then more, could it be?! "I love you" it read and I felt a chill,
for those three simple words, they knew me so well.

Someone special I knew must have sent this from above.
I miss them so much, but I can still feel their love.

I decided it was best if I pass it along,
I ran home for supplies - tape, glue and
ribbon, it needed to be strong!

One final quick addition, I added a name,
someone special to me, who I know feels the same.

I set off for the playground, the highest point I could climb,
I let go of the plane and it took off in no time.

As I walked home that day I saw
more and more fall. My heart was happy as
I realize it's love, being sent to us **all**.

Paper Airplanes of Love is a story that emphasizes love lost but never forgotten with the simplicity of a paper airplane. The plane catches the character's eye and remains with them until they are inspired to pass it along and spread love to others. The thought of a loved one always being with us is both innocent and pure, and as shown in this story – there will always be a way to embrace and share that feeling.

CUT OUT THE PAPER ON THE LINE AND FOLLOW THE INSTRUCTIONS BELOW TO MAKE YOUR OWN PAPER AIRPLANE!

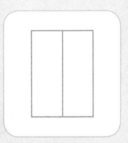

Fold paper
in half

Unfold and then fold the
corners into the center line

Fold the top edges
to the center

Fold the plane
in half

Fold down the wings to meet
the bottom edge of the plane's body

33233193R00017

Made in the USA
Lexington, KY
09 March 2019